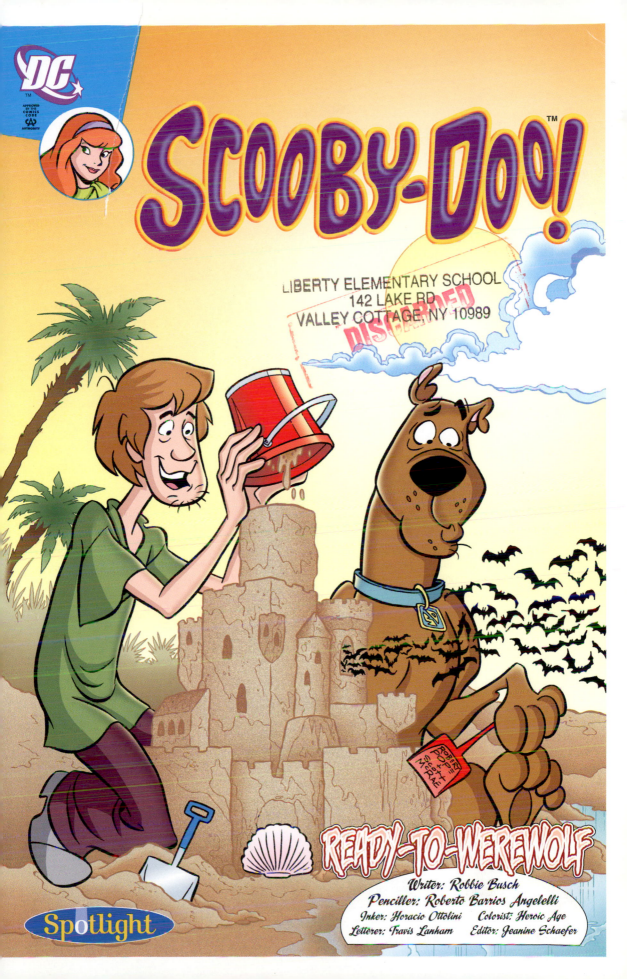

VISIT US AT
www.abdopublishing.com

Reinforced library bound edition published in 2010 by Spotlight, a division of the ABDO Group, 8000 West 78th Street, Edina, Minnesota 55439. Spotlight produces high-quality reinforced library bound editions for schools and libraries. Published by agreement with Warner Bros.—A Time Warner Company. All rights reserved. Used under authorization.

Printed in the United States of America, Melrose Park, Illinois.
092009
012010

Library of Congress Cataloging-in-Publication Data

Busch, Robbie.
 Scooby-Doo in Ready-to-werewolf / writer, Robbie Busch ; penciller, Roberto Barrios Angelelli ; inker, Horacio Ottolini ; colorist, Heroic Age ; letterer, Travis Lanham. -- Reinforced library bound ed.
    p. cm. -- (Scooby-Doo graphic novels)
 ISBN 978-1-59961-696-4
 I. Angelelli, Roberto Barrios. II. Scooby-Doo (Television program) III. Title. IV. Title: Ready-to-were-wolf.
 PZ7.7.B9Sf 2010
 741.5'973--dc22

                                    2009032901

All Spotlight books have reinforced library bindings and
are manufactured in the United States of America.

GOODNIGHT, JEAN PAUL. YOU REALLY SHOULD GET SOME REST, WE STILL HAVE A FEW DAYS BEFORE THE FASHION SHOW.

EH? OUI, OUI... GOODNIGHT, SAMZON. PLEAZE LOCK UP ON YOUR WAY OUT.

SAMZON! YOU ARE IN MY LIGHT! GO HOME AL--

AAARRRGGGHHH!!!

...READY! ZOOT ALORES! WHAT IZ ZIS MADNESS?!

CRASH
RIP
SHRED

READY-TO-WEREWOLF

Writer: Robbie Busch
Penciller: Roberto Barrios Angelelli
Inker: Horacio Ottolini   Colorist: Heroic Age
Letterer: Travis Lanham   Editor: Jeanine Schaefer

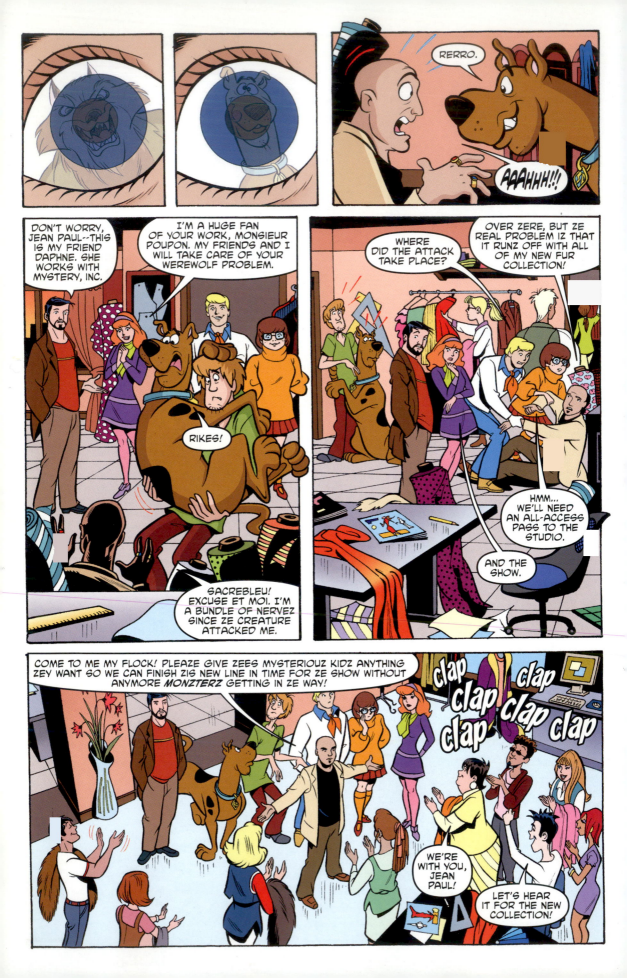

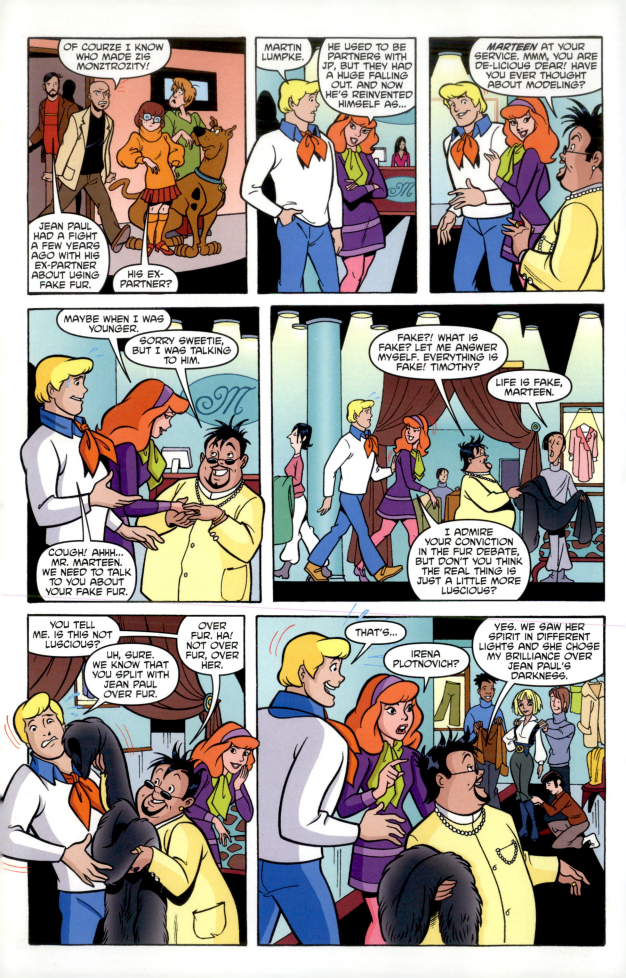

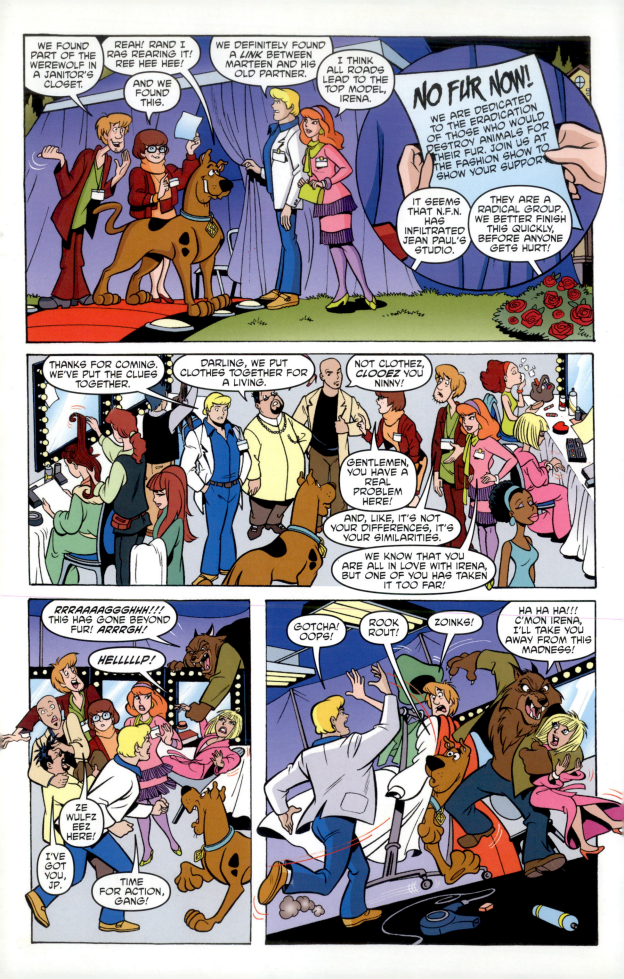

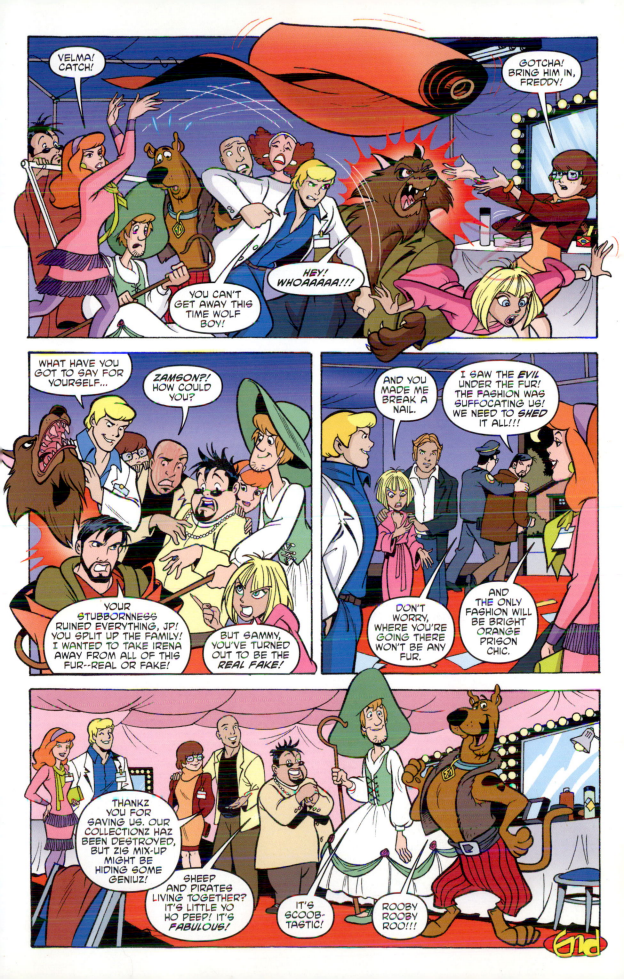

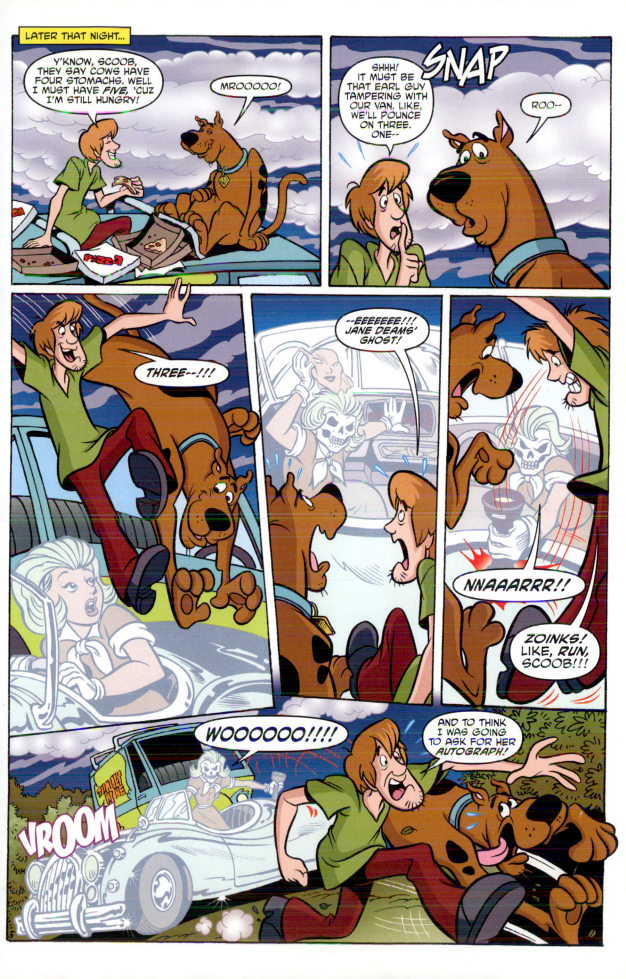

ZOINKS! FOLLOW THE RIGHT PATH TO GET SCOOBY AND SHAGGY BACK TO THEIR FRIENDS!

I WISH I HADN'T EATEN ALL THOSE PIZZAS!

WHAT WAS ALL THAT *RACKET*, SHAGGY?

≥pant-pant≤ LIKE, JANE DEAMS WAS TRYING TO *RUN US DOWN*!

I DON'T SEE ANY DEAD MOVIE STARS.

BELIEVE ME! SHE PULLED HER *FACE OFF*!

MAYBE SO, BUT THERE'S SOMETHING FISHY ABOUT THIS GHOST. I SUSPECT SHE'S MORE FLESH THAN PHANTOM.

SO YOU THINK IT MIGHT BE EARL IN DISGUISE?

ALL I KNOW IS, IF THIS GHOST FAILED TO GET US TONIGHT, THEN IT'S COMING FOR US TOMORROW. WE'LL HAVE TO STAY ON *OUR TOES.*

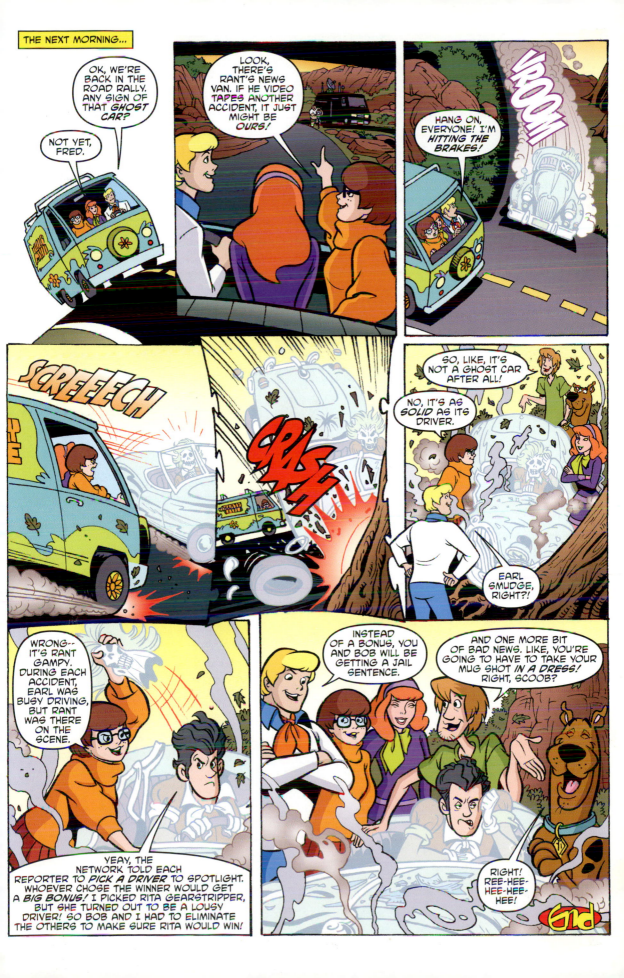

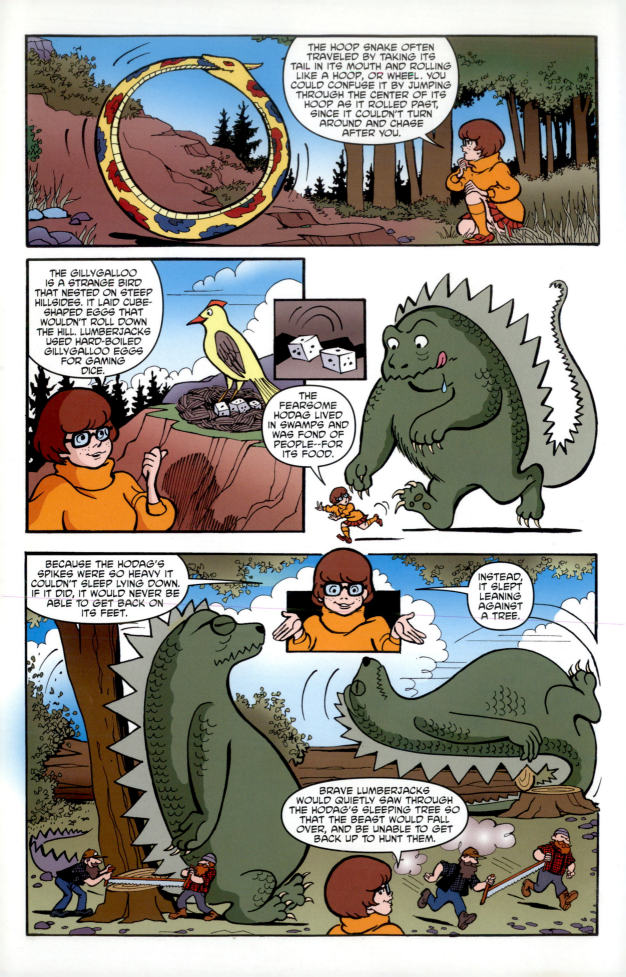

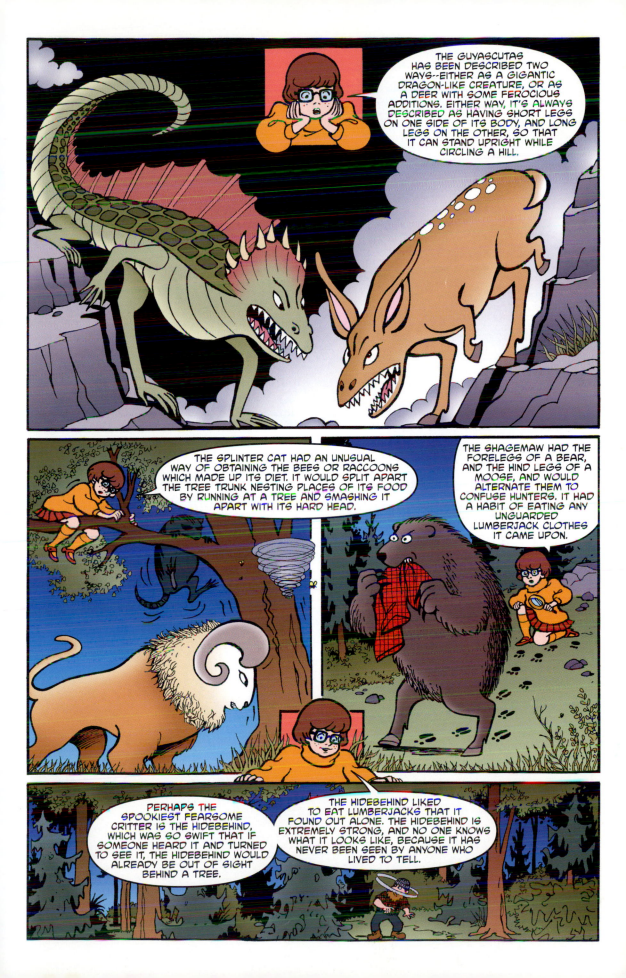